STATEHOOD DATES (Oldest to Youngest)

State	Date	State	Date
Delaware	December 7, 1787	Michigan	January 26, 1837
Pennsylvania	December 12, 1787	Florida	March 3, 1845
New Jersey	December 18, 1787	Texas	December 29, 1845
Georgia	January 2, 1788	Iowa	December 28, 1846
Connecticut	January 9, 1788	Wisconsin	May 29, 1848
Massachusetts	February 6, 1788	California	September 9, 1850
Maryland	April 28, 1788	Minnesota	May 11, 1858
South Carolina	May 23, 1788	Oregon	February 14, 1859
New Hampshire	June 21, 1788	Kansas	January 29, 1861
Virginia	June 25, 1788	West Virginia	June 20, 1863
New York	July 26, 1788	Nevada	October 31, 1864
North Carolina	November 21, 1789	Nebraska	March 1, 1867
Rhode Island	May 29, 1790	Colorado	August 1, 1876
Vermont	March 4, 1791	North Dakota	November 2, 1889
Kentucky	June 1, 1792	South Dakota	November 2, 1889
Tennessee	June 1, 1796	Montana	November 8, 1889
Ohio	March 1, 1803	Washington	November 11, 1889
Louisiana	April 30, 1812	Idaho	July 3, 1890
Indiana	December 11, 1816	Wyoming	July 10, 1890
Mississippi	December 10, 1817	Utah	January 4, 1896
Illinois	December 3, 1818	Oklahoma	November 16, 1907
Alabama	December 14, 1819	New Mexico	January 6, 1912
Maine	March 15, 1820	Arizona	February 14, 1912
Missouri	August 10, 1821	Alaska	January 3, 1959
Arkansas	June 15, 1836	Hawaii	August 21, 1959

Statehood dates are just like STATES' BIRTHDAYS!

HAPPY BIRTHDAY

Hey, Idaho—You and Laurie Keller have the same BIRTHDAY!

Hmmm, I wonder which one of us is older?

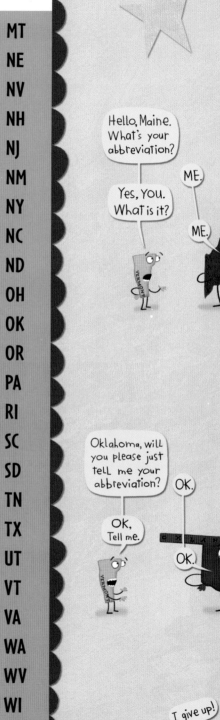

STATE ABBREVIATIONS

Alabama	AL	Montana	MT
Alaska	AK	Nebraska	NE
Arizona	AZ	Nevada	NV
Arkansas	AR	New Hampshire	NH
California	CA	New Jersey	NJ
Colorado	CO	New Mexico	NM
Connecticut	CT	New York	NY
Delaware	DE	North Carolina	NC
Florida	FL	North Dakota	ND
Georgia	GA	Ohio	OH
Hawaii	HI	Oklahoma	OK
Idaho	ID	Oregon	OR
Illinois	IL	Pennsylvania	PA
Indiana	IN	Rhode Island	RI
Iowa	IA	South Carolina	SC
Kansas	KS	South Dakota	SD
Kentucky	KY	Tennessee	TN
Louisiana	LA	Texas	TX
Maine	ME	Utah	UT
Maryland	MD	Vermont	VT
Massachusetts	MA	Virginia	VA
Michigan	MI	Washington	WA
Minnesota	MN	West Virginia	WV
Mississippi	MS	Wisconsin	WI
Missouri	MO	Wyoming	WY

For Christy— Thank you from the bottom of my little
ol' heart for your wisdom, inspiration, and humor for
the past 10 years. Here's to 10 more! —L. K.

THIS BOOK BELONGS TO:

WHO LIVES IN THE CITY OF:

IN THE COUNTY OF:

IN THE STATE OF:

A thank-you song to Christy Ottaviano
(to be sung to a tune by KC and the Sunshine Band):

When you edit my manuscripts and mark them up with your red pen,
You are cheery and friendly when you tell me to go try again.
I like the way, uh-huh, uh-huh, you edit, uh-huh, uh-huh.
Like the way, uh-huh, uh-huh, you edit, uh-huh, uh-huh.

Special thanks to Joanne Forth
for inspiring me to write about cities
and counties. Thanks, Joanne!

SQUARE FISH
An Imprint of Macmillan

THE SCRAMBLED STATES OF AMERICA TALENT SHOW. Copyright © 2008 by Laurie Keller. All rights reserved. Distributed in Canada by H.B. Fenn and Company Ltd.
Printed in May 2010 in China by South China Printing Co. Ltd., Dongguan City, Guangdong Province. For information, address Square Fish, 175 Fifth Avenue, New York, NY 10010.

Square Fish and the Square Fish logo are trademarks of Macmillan and
are used by Henry Holt and Company under license from Macmillan.

Library of Congress Cataloging-in-Publication Data
Keller, Laurie. / The scrambled states of America talent show / Laurie Keller.
p.   cm. / Companion to: The scrambled states of America.
Summary: The states decide to get together and put on a show featuring their particular talents. Includes facts about the history and geography of the states.
ISBN: 978-0-312-62824-6
1. U.S. states—Juvenile fiction. [1. U.S. states—Fiction. 2. Talent shows—Fiction.] I. Title. / PZ7.K281346Scr 2008 / [E]—dc22 / 2007040907

Originally published in the United States by Christy Ottaviano Books, an imprint of Henry Holt and Company
Square Fish logo designed by Filomena Tuosto
First Square Fish Edition: 2010
10 9 8 7 6 5 4 3 2 1
www.squarefishbooks.com

The illustrations were created using acrylic paint and collage on Arches watercolor paper and assembled in Photoshop on a Macintosh computer.
Laurie Keller consumed large amounts of coffee and M&Ms during the illustration process. Without them, this book might still not be completed.

I've never stung
a state before.

Go for it!

the

Scrambled States of America

Talent Show

by Laurie Keller

SQUARE
FISH

HENRY HOLT AND COMPANY

N E W   Y O R K

HELLO THERE.

I'm Sam. Please pardon the mess.

We're just cleaning up after the big—

WAIT, Uncle Sam! Don't spoil it!

You have to start from the **beginning!**

I'm Sweepin' to the Oldies!

HooVie

It all started quite simply, really.
In the middle of the night,
New York woke up from
a dream and shouted,

HEY, EVERYONE— LET'S HAVE A TALENT SHOW!

Did someone say

TALENT SHO

And quicker than you could say "Star-Spangled Banner," a talent show was under way! The states were so excited as they made their preparations. Some states planned solo acts and others planned group acts.

Some preferred to use their talents behind the scenes. Indiana was the director, Arizona was the costume designer, and a number of states worked as stagehands, setting up the stage, lights, sound, and props.

After a few days of blood, sweat, and tears,

the states were ready for the big show.

All the states, that is, except for Georgia. She was one of The Jolly Jugglers, along with California, Idaho, and Massachusetts. But every time they tried to rehearse, she'd start shaking so much she'd drop everything they tried to juggle.

I can't work with THIS! Get my agent on the phone!

"I'm worried about you, Georgia," Massachusetts said caringly. (Massachusetts is a very caring state.) "I think you should see the doctor." "I don't know what's wrong with me," said Georgia. "I'll make an appointment."

The next morning Georgia told Dr. Globe all about her shaking, so he decided to run some tests. He checked her square miles, temperature, and average yearly rainfall. "Now I'd like to take some X-rays. Don't worry, this won't hurt a bit," Dr. Globe assured her.

"First, a close look at your CITIES.

"Now, let's zoom out a bit and take a peek at your COUNTIES."

Dr. Globe finished the exam and looked over the results.

"Everything looks fine to me, Georgia. Tell me, is there anything *unusual* going on in your life?"

"Well, I'm in this talent show tonight and—"

The words were barely out of her mouth when suddenly she started shaking.

"That's IT!"

cried Dr. Globe.

"You've got a simple case of **STAGE FRIGHT!**"

"Stage fright?" asked Georgia.

"YES, it means you're nervous about performing in front of an audience."

"I *AM* nervous, Doc!" Georgia realized.

"Is there any cure for stage fright?"

"Well, the more you perform, the easier it gets. But for tonight you could try picturing the audience in their underwear."

"WHAT?!"

Georgia squawked.

"I know it sounds crazy, but it's supposed to make the audience seem less scary. Give it a try!"

That night the curtain opened to a bustling audience full of excited states waiting to perform.

"Ladies and Gentlemen, welcome to the first ever SCRAMBLED STATES TALENT SHOW! I'm your host—Washington, D.C.

He's the capital of our country, you know.

Yes, and he can also play the harmonica with his nose.

By the way, does anyone know what 'D.C.' stands for because I don't have a CLUE! HA!... heh, heh... ummm, yeah. **A N Y W A Y...** **ON WITH THE SHOW!"**

D.C. means District of Columbia.

I thought it meant Department of Cucumbers.

Washington, D.C., introduced the first act of the evening,
which happened to be the "First State" himself—Delaware.

I will now name all fifty states in order of their statehood while jumping on this pogo stick. Drum roll, please.

MYSELF, December 7, 1787...

Pennsylvania, December 12, 1787...

New Jersey, December 18, 1787...

Georgia, January 2, 1788...

WHOA!

Connecticut

January 9,

OOPS!

Sorry about that!

Next came Kentucky, who sang while playing the banjo,

Oregon, who sang while playing the organ,

and Ohio, who sang while Delaware tried to gain control of his pogo stick!

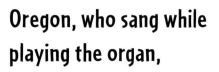

1788...

HELP!

Yikes!

SORRY!

Michigan's ventriloquist act was a winner. (Who's doing the talking, anyway?)

Hey, dummy, why don't you sing a song for everyone?

Who are you calling "dummy," dummy?

Minnesota the Magnificent wowed the crowd (with the help of his assistants).

The States on Skates kept the show rolling.

Hawaii and Kansas performed the hula,

Mississippi and Nevada danced the tango,

and just before intermission, The New States on the Block brought the audience to their feet!

Montana and the Montanettes kicked off the second half with their lively song and dance.

So when there's music and moonlight
and states and romance . . .
let's face the music and dance!

Pennsylvania played a peppy tune on the Liberty Bell, but when his song went on too long, Indiana, the director, started to panic.

I'll take care of it!

Oklahoma said confidently.
(Oklahoma is a very confident state.)

Alaska, the largest state, and Rhode Island, the smallest state, performed an act that had the audience on the edge of their seats.

Iowa's corny jokes and Wisconsin's cheesy sculptures got the crowd laughing,

I'LL tell ya what "IOWA" means. I went to the dentist today and now I-OWE-A lotta money!

It looks just like me!

and the State Impersonators had them rolling in the aisles!

I'm Oklahoma. What's up with this handle, anyway? I mean, what am I—a state or a FRYING PAN?

Hi, I'm Idaho. ALL I ever talk about is POTATOES-this and POTATOES-that...

POTATOES, POTATOES, POTATOES! Somebody stop me!

Oh, it hurts!

I DO love potatoes!

Well, the time had come for Georgia and the other Jolly Jugglers to take the stage. Georgia wasn't feeling particularly jolly. In fact, she'd never felt so S C A R E D in her life!

"You can DO it," Massachusetts whispered as they stood behind the curtain.

Georgia was just about to try Dr. Globe's suggestion when she heard Washington, D.C., say,

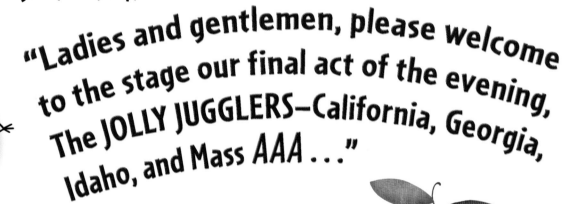

"Ladies and gentlemen, please welcome to the stage our final act of the evening, The JOLLY JUGGLERS—California, Georgia, Idaho, and Mass AAA . . ."

At that very moment, Washington, D.C., got a whiff of Georgia's peachy perfume and felt a sneeze the size of Alaska coming on.

 "Mass AAA . . .

Mass AAA . . ."

Just as the curtain started to rise, Washington, D.C., let out a sneeze so big that it blew Massachusetts

right off his feet!

Is that Europe over there?

Things seemed to move in SLOW MOTION as Massachusetts sailed through the air. In a panic, Indiana yelled to The Jolly Jugglers,

Start juggling!

START JUGGLING!

So they did!

I'm not used to all this SUSPENSE!

Gesundheit!

Georgia had no time now for stage fright. She was worried sick about Massachusetts when suddenly, as she stood there juggling,

he
landed
right
in
her
hands!

Nice catch!

And, as everyone in show business knows, if something unplanned happens, **the show must go on!** So she kept juggling. The states roared with delight—even Georgia.

I'm roaring with delight!

Me, too!

The show was such a success that Washington, D.C., invited EVERYONE up onstage for a

CELEBRATION!

Back at home, the states chatted for hours about their big night.

And even though Georgia didn't have to picture the audience in their underwear . . .

STATEHOOD DATES (Oldest to Youngest)

State	Date	State	Date
Delaware	December 7, 1787	Michigan	January 26, 1837
Pennsylvania	December 12, 1787	Florida	March 3, 1845
New Jersey	December 18, 1787	Texas	December 29, 1845
Georgia	January 2, 1788	Iowa	December 28, 1846
Connecticut	January 9, 1788	Wisconsin	May 29, 1848
Massachusetts	February 6, 1788	California	September 9, 1850
Maryland	April 28, 1788	Minnesota	May 11, 1858
South Carolina	May 23, 1788	Oregon	February 14, 1859
New Hampshire	June 21, 1788	Kansas	January 29, 1861
Virginia	June 25, 1788	West Virginia	June 20, 1863
New York	July 26, 1788	Nevada	October 31, 1864
North Carolina	November 21, 1789	Nebraska	March 1, 1867
Rhode Island	May 29, 1790	Colorado	August 1, 1876
Vermont	March 4, 1791	North Dakota	November 2, 1889
Kentucky	June 1, 1792	South Dakota	November 2, 1889
Tennessee	June 1, 1796	Montana	November 8, 1889
Ohio	March 1, 1803	Washington	November 11, 1889
Louisiana	April 30, 1812	Idaho	July 3, 1890
Indiana	December 11, 1816	Wyoming	July 10, 1890
Mississippi	December 10, 1817	Utah	January 4, 1896
Illinois	December 3, 1818	Oklahoma	November 16, 1907
Alabama	December 14, 1819	New Mexico	January 6, 1912
Maine	March 15, 1820	Arizona	February 14, 1912
Missouri	August 10, 1821	Alaska	January 3, 1959
Arkansas	June 15, 1836	Hawaii	August 21, 1959

Statehood dates are just like STATES' BIRTHDAYS!

HaPPY BiRTHDaY

Hey, Idaho—You and Laurie Keller have the same BiRTHDAY!

Hmmm, I wonder which one of us is older?

STATE ABBREVIATIONS

Alabama	AL	Montana	MT
Alaska	AK	Nebraska	NE
Arizona	AZ	Nevada	NV
Arkansas	AR	New Hampshire	NH
California	CA	New Jersey	NJ
Colorado	CO	New Mexico	NM
Connecticut	CT	New York	NY
Delaware	DE	North Carolina	NC
Florida	FL	North Dakota	ND
Georgia	GA	Ohio	OH
Hawaii	HI	Oklahoma	OK
Idaho	ID	Oregon	OR
Illinois	IL	Pennsylvania	PA
Indiana	IN	Rhode Island	RI
Iowa	IA	South Carolina	SC
Kansas	KS	South Dakota	SD
Kentucky	KY	Tennessee	TN
Louisiana	LA	Texas	TX
Maine	ME	Utah	UT
Maryland	MD	Vermont	VT
Massachusetts	MA	Virginia	VA
Michigan	MI	Washington	WA
Minnesota	MN	West Virginia	WV
Mississippi	MS	Wisconsin	WI
Missouri	MO	Wyoming	WY